This Little Tiger Book Belongs To:

_____

_____

_____

_____

LITTLE TIGER PRESS
An imprint of Magi Publications
1 The Coda Centre, 189 Munster Road,
London SW6 6AW
This paperback edition published 2002
First published in Great Britain 2000
Text © 2000 Sheridan Cain
Illustrations © 2000 Jack Tickle
ISBN 1 85430 641 3
3 5 7 9 10 8 6 4 2

The
Crunching Munching
Caterpillar

Sheridan Cain
Jack Tickle

LITTLE TIGER PRESS
London

Caterpillar was always hungry.
For weeks he crunched and munched
his way through the fresh,
juicy leaves of a blackberry bush.

Bzzzzzzzz

One day, Caterpillar was about to crunch into another leaf when . . .

Bzzzzzzzzzzz

Bumblebee landed beside him!

"Wow!" said Caterpillar,
"how did you get here?"
"Simple," said Bumblebee,
"I have wings. Look!"
"Oh, I'd like some of those,"
said Caterpillar.

Bumblebee flew up into the air and buzzed busily from flower to flower.

Bzzzzz

Bzzzz

"I'd love to fly like that," said Caterpillar.
"Well, you can't," said Bumblebee.
"I've got wings, and you've got legs. Your legs are for walking."
"I guess so," sighed Caterpillar.

Bzzzzzoommm

Bumblebee flew off to the next bush. Watching Bumblebee fly had made Caterpillar *very* hungry, so he crunched and he munched until it was time for bed.

crunch Munch
crunch Munch
yaw-w-n!

Caterpillar woke to
the sound of twittering.
Birds swooped and soared
in the early morning light.

Caterpillar was just about to start
his breakfast when . . .

Sparrow landed
beside him.

"I'd love to fly high in the air like that," said Caterpillar.
"Well, you can't," said Sparrow. "You need to be as light as the dandelion clock that floats on the breeze. You're far too fat to fly. Your legs are for walking."
"I guess so," said Caterpillar glumly.

Caterpillar carried on crunch-munching
all day, until the light began to dim.

Crunch
Munch

Crunch
Munch

He wrapped a leaf around himself to keep warm.
He was just about to go to sleep when . . .

Butterfly landed gracefully beside him.
"Oh, I wish I could fly like you," sighed Caterpillar.
"But I'm too fat and I have legs instead of wings."
Butterfly smiled a secret, knowing smile.
"Who knows? Perhaps one day you will fly,
light as a feather, like me," she said.
"But now, little Caterpillar, you should
go to sleep. You look very tired."

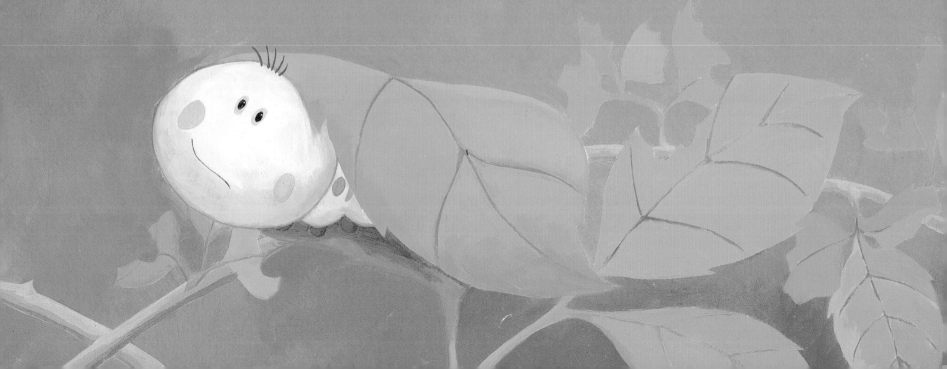

Butterfly was right. Caterpillar
suddenly felt very sleepy.
As Butterfly flew off into the
night sky, he fell into a deep,
deep sleep.

Caterpillar slept all through the winter,
and his sleep was filled with dreams.

He dreamed he had wings and was soaring in the blue sky above the tall trees . . . .

He dreamed he was a dandelion clock, drifting towards the sun.

He dreamed he was as light as a feather, floating on the breeze.

When Caterpillar woke up he felt
the warmth of the spring sun.
He was stiff from his long sleep,
but he did not feel very hungry.

He **stretched** and **stretched**...

and a breeze lifted
Caterpillar into the air.

He was no longer
short and plump.
He had WINGS!
Great, big, wonderful
BUTTERFLY WINGS!

"Wow!" said Young Butterfly. "I'm flying! I'm really flying!"

Munch your way through the latest treats
from Little Tiger Press

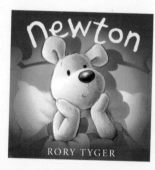

newton

RORY TYGER

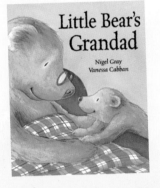

Little Bear's
Grandad

Nigel Gray
Vanessa Cabban

Fidgety Fish

Fireman
PiggyWiggy

Christyan and Diane Fox

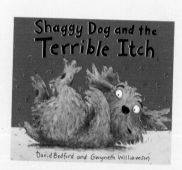

Shaggy Dog and the
Terrible Itch

David Bedford and Gwyneth Williamson

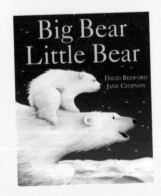

Big Bear
Little Bear

DAVID BEDFORD
JANE CHAPMAN

For information regarding any of the above
titles or for our catalogue, please contact us:
Little Tiger Press, 1 The Coda Centre,
189 Munster Road, London SW6 6AW, UK
Telephone: 020 7385 6333
Fax: 020 7385 7333
e-mail: info@littletiger.co.uk
www.littletigerpress.com

Is it my
turn?

David Bedford
and Elaine Field

Laura's
Christmas
Star

Klaus Baumgart

The Very
Noisy Night

Diana Hendry   Jane Chapman